CHAPTER 2

MOUSEKIN'S
GOLDEN HOUSE

MOUSEKIN'S GOLDEN HOUSE

STORY AND PICTURES BY EDNA MILLER

Simon and Schuster Books for Young Readers
Published by Simon & Schuster Inc., New York

Published by Simon and Schuster Books for Young Readers,
A Division of Simon & Schuster, Inc.,
Simon & Schuster Building, Rockefeller Center
1230 Avenue of the Americas, New York, NY 10020

10 9 8 7 6 5 4 3 2 1

30 29 28 27 26 25 24   pbk

Simon and Schuster Books for Young Readers
is a trademark of Simon & Schuster, Inc.
Manufactured in the U.S.A.

Library of Congress Cataloging-in-Publication Data
Miller, Edna, 1920–
    Mousekin's golden house.

    SUMMARY: A whitefoot mouse makes a home for the
winter in a jack-o'-lantern discarded after Halloween.
    [1. Mice—Fiction.   2. Pumpkin—Fiction.
3. Jack-o-lanterns—Fiction.]   I. Title.
PZ7.M6128Mo 1987 [E]   87-32111
ISBN 0-13-604232-5
ISBN 0-671-66972-9 pbk

In the woods
there are many tall trees,
and small trees
that reach to grow tall
in the deep shade.
There are low-growing bushes
with berries and seeds
that pop and roll
about the forest floor.

Beneath them all
are tiny paths
that only mice can see.

One moonlit night,
Mousekin followed just such a path
to one of his homes
in the chestnut log.

And right in the middle
of that very small path,
Mousekin saw *something*
that someone had thrown away
when Hallowe'en was over.

He hid behind a log.
Perhaps "it" was dangerous.

Mousekin had never seen a jack-o'-lantern
in all his mouse-days.
He wriggled his nose furiously
at the strange pumpkin smell.
He was so excited that he drummed
his tiny paw on the hollow log.

Mousekin was so interested in the jack-o'-lantern
that he did not watch for danger with his bright,
shoe-button eyes. Nor did he turn his large ears
to the breeze to listen for the sound of wings —
for owls and hawks and other creatures who wait
to catch a whitefoot mouse.

Suddenly, as Mousekin
made a second turn
around the smiling face,
a hungry, young owl
swooped toward him.

But, before the bird
could even blink its eyes,
Mousekin jumped straight
into the
jack-o'-lantern's mouth!

Once inside, he looked about.
He was in a beautiful golden room —
just the right size for a little mouse.

From one of the top windows
of his new room, Mousekin could see
the owl sulking in an evergreen tree.
The first rays of the morning sun
showed in the sky behind the owl.
Night was over,
and it was time
for Mousekin to go to sleep.

Mousekin felt safe
inside the sturdy walls
of his golden house.
He did not awaken until evening
when the Katydids began to argue —
"Katydid!" "Katy didn't!"

After he had stretched
and cleaned his white undercoat,
he began to explore his new home,
scurrying in one window and out another.
Now Mousekin was alert
to all the sounds
that filled the woods
when evening came.

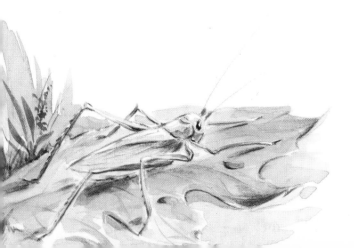

He heard a rustle in the bayberry bush,
and a soft step on the dry autumn leaves.
He knew it was the cat.
Just as the cat was about to spring,
Mousekin dove into the pumpkin
and began to houseclean.
Out of all the windows
flew bits of candle and pumpkin seeds.

The cat jumped —
but not for Mousekin.
He jumped straight up, and then ran
as fast as he could to get away
from the big round face
with the terrible teeth.
The cat would never
take that path through the woods again.

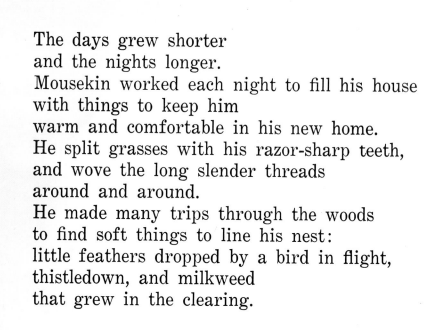

The days grew shorter
and the nights longer.
Mousekin worked each night to fill his house
with things to keep him
warm and comfortable in his new home.
He split grasses with his razor-sharp teeth,
and wove the long slender threads
around and around.
He made many trips through the woods
to find soft things to line his nest:
little feathers dropped by a bird in flight,
thistledown, and milkweed
that grew in the clearing.

While Mousekin was busy
gnawing and nibbling,
and doing all the things that mice do,
he still found time
to watch the animals
that passed by his golden house.
One very chilly evening,
a box turtle plodded by.
He never looked up or down,
but moved like a toy being pulled
to the pond at the edge of the wood,
to some tangled tree root beneath the ground,
where he would sleep away the winter months.

But when the turtle reached the jack-o'-lantern,
he stopped in his tracks and stretched his neck
to see if what he saw was true. Just then, Mousekin
popped his head out of one of his windows.

...And then...

the box turtle lost no time
in turning around
and heading once again
for the tangled root
beneath the ground,
near the pond,
at the edge of the wood.

Most of the birds
had gone to warmer lands.
Only the phoebe
was left in the thistle.

The wind blew hard now,
scooping up piles of leaves
and scattering them about
like hundreds of bright-winged birds.

One day the phoebe called to Mousekin:
"Come South with me,
Come right away.
Your house will never do.
The wind will blow,
The snow will snow,
And chill you
Through and through."

The little mouse
whistled a high soft "Goodbye!"
He would not leave
his golden house.

A chipmunk hurried by,
his mouth so full of nuts
he could hardly speak:
"Come with me,
Beneath the ground.
That house will never do.
The wind will blow,
The snow will snow,
And chill you
Through and through."

Mousekin scrambled up his golden house
and slipped through a tiny opening at the top.

He slid down the feathery stairway,
to the warm, soft lining below.

Mousekin curled up,
tucked his tiny feet beneath him,
wrapped his long tail
around some milkweed-down,
and pulled it closely around him,
and fell fast asleep.

Little by little and bit by bit
something happened to the jack-o'-lantern.
It began to close its eyes
in the frosty air.
It shut its mouth
against the cold wind.

The next day,
the gray sky opened
and great white flakes
fell upon the sleeping pumpkin.

Inside, Mousekin was curled up
into a tiny fur ball.
He was safe and warm,
and fast asleep
in his golden house.

E
Mil

Miller, Edna
Mousekin's golden
house
$ 9.95

DATE DUE	BORROWER'S NAME	ROOM NUMBER
	P Pastor	
OCT 2 1992	Stefanie	2
OCT 1 2 1993	Bonnie	6
OCT 1 5 1993	Bonnie	6

E
Mil

Miller, Edna
Mousekin's golden
house
$ 9.95